Books for All Foundation
Publishing Quality Accessible and
Inclusive Literature
Designed to Meet the Needs of All
Children!

I Am Grace

Written and illustrated by Stacey Adams

Published by:
Books for All Foundation
7709 W. 148th Street
Overland Park, KS 66223

Published in the United States of America

ISBN: 978-0-98362-360-1
Library of Congress Control Number: 2011908961

www.booksforallonline.com

Dedication

This book is dedicated to Grace and her wonderful family.
Their amazing story of love and acceptance is an inspiration to all.

My name is Grace.
I am like you.

I have a family.
I have a Mom and Dad.
I have three brothers.

I go to school.
I learn to read and write.

I like to play.
I dress-up and pretend.

I like animals.
I visit the pet store.

I like art.
I paint and color with crayons.

I like recess.
I play hide and seek.

My name is Grace.

I am different, too.

I have Down Syndrome.

I like you.
I want to talk to you.

I wear glasses.
I want to see you.

I listen.
I want to hear you.

I like you.
I want to play with you.

My name is Grace.

Who are you?

Afterword

Learn More: Down Syndrome

All people carry a special set of instructions inside their bodies called chromosomes. Chromosomes carry the information that makes us who we are. Each of us typically has twenty-three pairs of chromosomes. They determine everything about us: hair and eye color, height, and even medical conditions we might have. Down Syndrome is an example of one of these medical conditions. When this occurs, a person has three, rather than two, copies of the 21st chromosome.

This change in the body's instructions creates unique physical, medical and learning challenges for a person with Down Syndrome. For example, you may notice that a friend with Down Syndrome has a hard time talking or playing the way you do. If this is the case with your friend, try different ways of talking and playing together.

People with Down Syndrome typically have some degree of learning difficulty. This means they may learn at a slower pace or in a different way than you do. That's okay; each of us is different. We all have strengths and talents that make our relationships special. Remember patience, understanding, and a kind smile can make all the difference in the world. Taking the time to share these qualities is what makes our friendships meaningful!